NERO
CORLEONE

NERO CORLEONE
· A CAT'S STORY ·

By Elke Heidenreich

Translated by Doris Orgel

Illustrated by Quint Buchholz

VIKING

VIKING
Published by the Penguin Group
Penguin Putnam Inc., 375 Hudson Street, New York, New York 10014, U.S.A.
Penguin Books Ltd, 27 Wrights Lane, London W8 5TZ, England
Penguin Books Australia Ltd, Ringwood, Victoria, Australia
Penguin Books Canada Ltd, 10 Alcorn Avenue, Toronto, Ontario, Canada M4V 3B2
Penguin Books (N.Z.) Ltd, 182-190 Wairau Road, Auckland 10, New Zealand

Penguin Books Ltd, Registered Offices: Harmondsworth, Middlesex, England

First published in 1997 by Viking, a member of Penguin Putnam Inc.

1 3 5 7 9 10 8 6 4 2

Copyright © Carl Hanser Verlag Munchen Wien, 1995
Translation copyright © Penguin Putnam Inc., 1997
Translated by Doris Orgel
All rights reserved

Originally published in German under the title *Nero Corleone: Eine Katzengeschichte* by
Carl Hanser Verlag.

LIBRARY OF CONGRESS CATALOGING-IN-PUBLICATION DATA
Heidenreich, Elke.
[Nero Corleone. English]
Nero Corleone : a cat story / by Elke Heidenreich ; [illustrated
by Quint Buchholz] ; translated by Doris Orgel.   p. cm.
Summary : A bold and self-serving tom cat reigns supreme both in the farmyard
in Italy where he was born and later in the comfortable home in Germany
to which a vacationing couple takes him and his helpless sister.
ISBN 0-670-87395-0 (hc)
[1. Cats—Fiction.] I. Buchholz, Quint, ill. II. Orgel, Doris.
III. Title.
PZ7.H36155Ni 1997 [Fic]—dc21 97-12238 CIP AC

Printed in Singapore
Set in Waldbaum

For Leonie

Madonnina had lived on the farm for so long that nobody knew how old she was. Ten? Twelve? Sixteen? Or maybe only eight? She owed her name to the bright red patch of fur on top of her head with its part straight down the middle, just like a Madonna in an old painting.

Twice a year, every spring and fall, Madonnina had kittens, and if the farmer found them in their hiding place in time, he drowned them. "In time" meant before they opened their eyes and came toddling out behind their mother. Because after that he couldn't bring himself to do it.

"*Troppi gatti! Troppi gatti!*" he'd exclaim (that means, "Too many cats! Too many cats!"), and let them live. He'd find homes on other farms for as many as he could. The ones he couldn't give away, he somehow managed to feed along with the other cats on the farm. They included:

Paolo, a black-gray tiger-striped tom so old he had hardly any teeth left in his mouth.

Handsome Felix, all pearl gray, very elegant, but missing an eye. Back when he was young and saucy, the hens had scratched it out.

Red Messalina.

And Biff and Baff, two ever-hungry hooligans who kept the farm rat- and mouse-free.

They were joined, once or twice a year, by one or more of Madonnina's kittens. If it was a strong one it got along, and everything was in order.

The boss of the whole farm was the sulky old dog.

The hens, though not too bright, knew how to discourage anyone—remember what had happened to Handsome Felix—who annoyed them by trying to steal eggs right out from underneath them.

That's how it was, or as the tough little cat Madonnina liked to say, "Everything in its proper order."

Until one fateful Friday—Friday, November seventeenth.

But first you must know that in Italy, where our story begins, Friday the seventeenth is a dangerous, bad-luck day, like Friday the thirteenth in other countries: a day of lost wallets, missed kisses, and pimples on the nose. Moreover, November is the bad-luck month in Italy. And so, when the seventeenth of November falls on a Friday, and when, on top of all that, on this very day a darkly glowering sky hurls down a winter thunderstorm with hailstones as big as cherries, then it bodes very ill indeed.

On such a day Madonnina gave birth to four kittens—and among them, for the first time ever, was a pitch-black one. No, not totally black—the right forepaw was white. But that was all. It was *un maschio*, a male, a boy, a tom. A black tomcat, born on Friday the seventeenth of November, in thunder and lightning at twelve o'clock, high noon—oh dear! They named him Nero. Nero means "black."

One evening in early December, in his usual way, the farmer set down a big metal platter of noodles, rice, bread, milk, and a little bit of meat for his cats. This was when he first saw the four new kittens. Madonnina had brought them with her and had fought for places for them at the rim of the plate.

"*Porco dio!*" yelled the farmer. "*Quattro! E un nero!*" The curse I'd rather not translate, but the rest means, "Four! And a black one!"

In the next few weeks he found a home for the

two gray and white tiger-striped ones. A friend up in the mountains happily took them, for his barn was full of mice, and he figured two strong young cats could earn their keep by hunting.

The little red and white one the farmer named Rosa. She looked a lot like Madonnina. But she seemed awkward at the feeding plate and generally a bit slow. Well, he'd leave her with her mother for a while longer, then he'd see. Another thing about Rosa: she had sky-blue eyes and a funny squint, so you could never tell, was she looking at the metal plate or watching the clouds go by?

As for Nero, the black one, the farmer could never get hold of him. Whenever he bent down to scoop him up, whoosh, he was gone, fast as lightning, nowhere to be found.

"*Furbo!*" yelled the farmer, "Scoundrel!" and "*Diavolo nero!*" "Black devil!" But he could never catch him. The animals on the farm held their breath and said, "Who knows how things will go?"

They did not go well.

In no time at all Nero had everything and everyone firmly in hand, or rather, in his little white paw with the knife-sharp claws.

The hens provided him with one fresh egg daily of their own free will—this after he had opened his mouth up wide, flashed his pointy teeth, and hissed: "Or else I can chase you all over the place for longer than you can imagine, and you won't even have time to lay an egg." He had bristled his long white whiskers at them. And to show that he meant business, he had gone right up to Camilla, the bravest of them, and ripped a few feathers from her chest. Then they were scared and began cooperating gladly.

Every day he cracked his fresh egg open on a stone, slurped it down with noisy gusto, and purred, squeezing his poison-green, round-as-marbles eyes together into tiny slits. But even with his eyes closed, he never missed a thing. Every time, when he'd almost finished, he called Rosa and let her eat the rest. She always sat, not far away but at a respectful distance, admiring him, and waited humbly for her turn, and he never forgot her. It seemed to be his one good quality: his caring for dumb little Rosa. He protected her, gave her tastes of whatever he hunted, brought her down from up in the hay where otherwise she might have napped till past suppertime, and made sure she got her place at the metal dish. Also, he showed a certain respect for his mother, Madonnina—at least he never lifted a paw against her.

But the dog, boss over everyone else, had no clout with him. For two days Nero had observed him from an appropriate distance, taken his measure, studied the length and reach of his chain, and carefully considered his bared teeth. On the third day, not making a sound, he'd stolen over. The old dog didn't even hear him coming, just kept dozing till a small paw—the white one!—carefully covered his left eye.

"It's me," said Nero. "Don't even bother to bark. I want you to think about something. Pay attention: *This* is what it's like to see with only *one* eye."

"What do you mean?" growled the old dog, his free eye blinking at this little pitch-black imp. He felt greatly troubled. No cat had ever dared treat him this way.

"What I mean," said Nero softly, "is that you can't see as much with one eye as with two. So, if you show off by barking, growling, or any other nonsense, or wake me up when I'm napping in the sun, then I'll just go like this—" He sank one claw into the tender skin right near the dog's eye, and the poor old dog howled loudly. "Then, very likely, that eye will be gone, and you'll have, as I said, only one. Just so you know. I'm glad we understand each other. *Buon giorno* [which means good day]." And he was gone again.

The other animals held their breath. The hen Camilla sighed and said, "Madonnina, what did you hatch us here?"

Madonnina polished her short, three-colored fur and said, "First, a mother loves all her children equally. And, second, why do you put up with it? He

doesn't try any of his little antics with *me*." Then she looked on as Nero jumped straight onto the windowsill and into the kitchen for some mouthfuls of a vanilla pudding that had been put there to cool, and she purred, "Oh, somehow I find him sweet, little scamp though he may be."

"Being rude, extorting eggs, you call that sweet?" clucked the hens, enraged.

And the sheep said, "He jumps right up and naps on our woolly backs, and we can't shake him off. Baah!"

The old donkey groaned, "Ever since he's been here, he's been causing so much commotion that I can't manage to do any profound thinking. Two weeks ago I thought of something really important, and now I don't even remember what it was. It might have been a revelation about what it is deep, deep down that holds the whole world together. But I can't remember a thing; it's all gone. I can't concentrate anymore."

Messalina scowled. "Ever since he's been here, the rest of us can't eat our fill; he grabs most of the food right off the dish."

And the old farm dog muttered, "If I ever catch that Satan, I'll bite him right—" Right in

15

two, he wanted to say, but the farmer's wife had thrown a slipper at Nero, and all of a sudden the little black fireball stood snarling before the dog. The dog cleared his throat as though from a coughing fit, and just to be on the safe side, said, "Um, right around now, in the middle of winter, my throat always feels scratchy!"

So the weeks went by, and then it was the day before New Year's. On top of the hill across from the farm stood a small vacation house belonging to a couple from Germany. These two people arrived in a big old car with suitcases full of books several times a year—in spring, at the beginning of summer, in mild autumn, or sometimes over Christmas and New Year's. Then the shutters of the house flew open, and the windows, too, to let in air. Smoke rose up from the chimney if it was winter, and in summer two lounge chairs appeared in the little garden. And the couple sat by the fire or lay in the lounge chairs reading the books they had brought. When they had read all the books, they waved good-bye to the farmer, and drove back to Germany. Sometimes during their stay, they crossed the meadow, chatted with the farmer—about the

weather, politics, and Lothar Matthäus, the most famous soccer player in all of Europe. Sometimes the
farmer brought them a head of lettuce and fresh
herbs from his garden. Sometimes the couple gave
him a bottle of white Rhine wine. And sometimes
Madonnina went to visit them, slinking up the
stairs and all around the house, and got a little
saucer of milk.

"Aha, something's happening," Nero saw right
away on New Year's Eve morning, as soon as
the shutters came open. Half an hour later, smoke
welled up from the chimney, and the air smelled of
wood fire. Even so, the windows stayed wide open.
And Nero ran through the wilted wintry meadow
up toward the house, jumped onto the window
ledge, and, seeing nobody inside, jumped into the
living room.

He had never been in a living room before,
and he looked at everything very carefully. First he
checked for possible sources of danger: Were there
hens with sharp beaks? Any dogs? Someone who
might throw a slipper at him? Noises came from the
next room, as though somebody was rummaging
around in there. But here in the spacious living

room, except for the soft crackling of the fire in the fireplace, a beautiful silence reigned.

For the first time in his tomcat life, Nero stepped on a carpet—a soft pink carpet with a design of small green vines. Carefully he placed his paws, sank in a little, stretched, made himself lo-o-o-o-ong, and sharpened his claws in the wool, *scritch scratch*, thereby pulling out a couple of carpet threads. Hmm, he liked that. And he went along the whole edge of the carpet, scratching, *scritchy scratchy*, all the way to the couch.

It was a green couch with thick pink pillows. Nero stood on his hind legs and tested it with his forepaws: good, very good, very nice and soft, almost as soft as the hay over on the farm and not as prickly. In one leap he was up there; he turned around a few times and rolled himself up on the pillows.

Stop a moment, please. Imagine how high a couch is, and how small a cat is. A cat taking such a leap would be comparable to a man jumping from a standing position, with no running start, up to the roof of his house, or to the second-floor balcony.

Yes, cats are a wonder—and not just because of leaps like that. Cats, even when they're sleeping, can hear a mouse's softest squeak. Cats can see in the pitch dark, and they never need glasses. Cats don't make a sound when they walk. They have thick, soft fur, and they don't sweat, even in the sun. They can run over jagged stones, blazing hot pavement, and frozen fields without hurting their delicate, soft paws, and when necessary, they can shoot out their claws, sharp as little switchblades. Cats can fall into the mud and, ten minutes later, look as neat and proper as if they had just had a bath. Cats can scoot straight up a tree and in one bound leap down again, as though there was nothing to it. And when they feel good, they can let an indescribable sound come rollicking forth from their throats—a sound somewhere between that of a distant thunderstorm rumbling, a small van far away in the night rolling over a wooden bridge, and a teakettle seconds before the water boils, just beginning to buzz. It is one of the loveliest sounds in the world, and it is called purring.

Nero purred.

He lay on the green upholstery, leaning against pink pillows, and purred. He could hear very well that someone was approaching from the next room, but he didn't feel like giving up this paradise to jump up and rush away. He felt entitled to lie here, and if anyone disagreed—well, he could always count on his dangerous, lightning-quick claws.

He narrowed his eyes to slits and watched a blond-haired woman stuffing a pile of clothes into a dresser drawer. She pushed a strand of hair away from her face and put her hand on her aching back as she straightened up and—

"*Now!*" thought Nero. "Now she'll turn around; now I must stay motionless, be watchful, *pay attention!*"

The woman turned, and looked at him, but, as Nero saw instantly, she did not seem unfriendly. She was only half as fat as the farmer's wife. She had blue eyes and gazed, surprised, and—as Nero noticed—admiringly at the little black guest amidst her pillows.

Nero shot to his feet, ready to play the game of "Who-might-*you*-be?" He made his green eyes round as though with fright, stared into the woman's eyes, opened his cute little pink mouth, and uttered the pitiful, heart-melting *meee-oow!* that he had practiced so carefully on many a boring afternoon. It did not fail to achieve its effect.

"Well, and who might *you* be?" asked the blond-haired woman, quite taken, and carefully came nearer.

"Oh for Pete's sake," Nero thought, "who might I be, who might I be? It's as plain as daylight. I'm a black tomcat, that's who." And he trustingly stretched out his paws toward her.

The woman knelt down in front of the couch and stroked him.

"Oh, but you're a sweet little fellow," she said. "Where did you come from, all of a sudden?"

"Most likely I flew in through the window," said Nero, nestling his black little head in her arm, in her hand, and making loud mewing noises.

"Are you hungry?" asked the woman, standing up.

"Yesyesyes!" he exclaimed, for, as it happened, he was always hungry, or, shall we say, always in the mood to eat. And all of a sudden he knew: "This blond-haired woman's a pushover! I can twist her around my paw!"

The woman went into the kitchen. Instantly Nero sprang from the couch, trotted after her, rubbed against her leg, and kept on mewing as soul-stirringly as he could.

She opened the refrigerator, took out a can, and poured a little condensed milk into a saucer. She added a little warm water from the faucet and stirred it with her index finger. "There. That way it won't be too cold for your dear little belly."

"'Dear little belly,' my paw!" thought Nero. "Hurry up, don't take all day, put that saucer down!" And he stood up tall on his hind legs, begging so hard with his forepaws that it made the blond-haired woman, leaning toward him, spill a few drops from the saucer.

Even before it stood firmly on the kitchen tiles, Nero dipped his pink tongue in and lapped and gulped.

"My, but you're impatient," said the woman, laughing. And Nero thought, "Who did you think I was? Holy, patient Saint Anthony?" and licked the saucer shiny clean.

The blond-haired woman went back into the living room and called, "Robert, come see what a dear little guest we have!"

"Robert? Who might this Robert be?" Nero wondered with some misgivings, remembering the farmer furiously hurling galoshes at him.

Robert was as tall as a tree, wearing thick glasses, and he had a cigar in his mouth. As this person came into the kitchen, Nero quickly glanced around and mapped out an escape route for himself.

"Where did *he* come from?" said Robert, in a not-too-friendly way.

"He was lying on the couch," the woman answered. "The poor little fellow was hungry, so I gave him a little milk."

"If he's hungry, you should give him some real food," said Robert. "Isn't there anything left of the sausage sandwich we brought?"

"Robert, you're all right," thought Nero, pleased.

"Sausage sandwich?" said the woman. "Cats don't eat sausage sandwiches!"

"Oh no? The bread part you can keep," thought Nero. "Just hand over the sausage, quick!" And he uttered a long, exceedingly mournful mee-eee-ow.

"You see, he's hungry," said Robert. "Go on, try giving him some."

"What makes you think it's a he?" the woman asked, groping around in a bag that stood, still unpacked, on the kitchen table.

"He's a tomcat, I can see." Robert bent down, blew disgusting cigar smoke into Nero's face, and looked under his tail. Nero gave an angry screech. "Yes, a tomcat," Robert said.

Meanwhile the woman had unwrapped part of a sandwich and crumbled it into the saucer. Nero got a whiff of good German pork sausage. With his right forepaw, the white one, he pushed the bits of bread to the side, licking off an occasional bit of butter, and busied himself with the small, round, pink pork sausage morsels. *Swoop*, the first, *hup*, the second, *swup*, the third, *smack*, the fourth—yum!

"My goodness, how he can eat!" said the blond-haired woman, delighted, and knelt down to pet him.

"Now you'll never be rid of him," Robert muttered darkly.

Nero was still thinking about what Robert had said long after he returned to the farm. All the time the New Year's Eve fireworks were blasting off down in the village, all the time he lay in the hay cuddling with Rosa while she licked and polished his fur as she did every night, that sentence of Robert's lingered in Nero's ears.

Smelling of milk and pork sausage, he tried to give her hints of a better, more gracious life, a life that one could spend on soft carpets and in warm, cozy couch corners, a life where saucers were always full and people ready to admire one for being special, a wonderfully accomplished creature, instead of just an ordinary, barely tolerated farm cat.

Nero told in great detail of his visit to the German couple, what daring it had taken to jump up onto the couch of total strangers like that. News of it spread like wildfire, and soon everyone on the farm was calling him Lionheart. *Cuore di leone* is

how you say it in Italian, or as a name, Corleone, Nero Corleone . . . "Preceded by Don"—which means "sir"—"if you please!" he requested, and so that became his name.

"Don?" cried the hens. "But you only say 'Don' to the priest and to important dignitaries—"

"And what do you think *I* am, a clown?" he demanded, puffing himself up to look big and important, and that was that. Don Nero Corleone he remained. And he was only six weeks old.

On New Year's morning the windows of the vacation house on the hill stayed closed a long time. But when, around eleven o'clock, the shutters were opened, Nero said to dumb little Rosa with the blue-eyed squint, "Come with me!"

And they made their way together in the cold January sunshine through the damp meadow over to the German couple's property.

"You wait here!" said Nero. He sat Rosa down underneath a pine bush and leaped onto the window ledge and stared through the windowpane into the living room.

The couple were sitting at a round table eating

breakfast. Robert glanced toward the window. "Hmm, just as I suspected. Isolde, look who's here!"

Isolde gave a little cry, whirled around, rushed to the window, and pushed it open so vehemently that Nero almost fell off the ledge. And Rosa, panicking, ran back across the meadow as fast as she could.

"Here you are again, my little darling," Isolde cooed, and lifted Nero into the room. "What would you say, I wonder, to a little bitty egg?"

"A little bitty egg, a little bitty milk, a little bitty sausage, by all means, give me all those good things, hurry up, hop to it," thought Nero, all the while making pathetic little hunger noises, acting as adorable as he possibly could. Meanwhile he kept a watchful eye on Robert. He couldn't quite gauge his attitude toward tomcats. But Isolde's heart he'd conquered, he knew that.

She took her own soft-boiled egg out of its eggcup, carefully peeled off the shell, put it in a saucer, mashed it up, and offered it to Nero.

"There. Do you like that?"

Nero tried it, and found, "Yes, I do." It tasted delicious; it was in a completely different class from the raw eggs over on the farm. He savored every lick and bite.

"But Isolde, now *you* don't have any egg," said Robert, enjoying his.

"Then give her yours, you miser," Nero would have liked to say. Suddenly he thought of Rosa, dear, fat, stupid Rosa who so enjoyed eating, and who was waiting for him out in the cold. He leaped back onto the window seat and with plaintive meowing noises scratched at the pane.

"What's wrong, darling?" called Isolde, startled. "You didn't even finish your little egg!"

And Robert said, "If he wants out, let him go."

"A reasonable man," thought Nero and sprang out the opened window into the cold garden.

No Rosa.

"Where are you, silly?" he cried, but she wasn't there. Furious, he dashed over toward the farm. Then he saw her sitting there, and she came toddling toward him, all timid, and sniffed at his whisker hairs.

"Why did you run away when I told you to stay put?" he growled. "Come on, let's go!" He made her run back across the meadow. "Hurry up, Fatso.

They have delicious eggs! And I saved you something special. *Avanti*, come on!"

"I'm too scared," mewed Rosa when Nero once again jumped up onto the window ledge.

"But you're coming, this instant," he hissed. "And when we're inside, just leave things to me."

"Isolde, look!" said Robert. "Now there's two of them!"

Isolde saw two little faces at the window: the familiar bold black one, and a shy red, white, and light gray one, round as a ball, with squinting bright blue eyes.

"How indescribably adorable!" she cried, and ran to the window and opened it, but this time very carefully, because Rosa looked so fearful. In fact, Rosa was just about to run away again, but Nero gave her a little shove which landed her inside on the soft carpet. He sprang in behind her and headed straight for the egg saucer.

"You, too," he said to Rosa. "Come on, Pudgie, have some. Don't worry, they won't hurt you. They think you're adorable."

Carefully and fearfully, but encouraged by Nero and enticed by the delicious aroma, little round Rosa came toward the saucer with the flower pattern. So now there they both stood, with their two furry heads bending over their soft-boiled egg breakfast, while Robert, concealing how charmed he was, and Isolde, close to tears of delight, looked on.

"Three-colored cats are lucky," Isolde murmured.

And Robert said, "Black cats are unlucky," which Isolde dismissed as a stupid superstition.

Rosa wanted to leave right then and go back home.

"No way," said Nero, licking the last bit of egg yolk off the saucer. "Now we lie down on the couch that I told you about."

"He brought his little girlfriend over," said Isolde. "That's *so* sweet."

"She looks cross-eyed to me," Robert muttered.

Tail held high, Nero strode to the couch. Rosa followed, making squeaky noises like a frightened little piglet.

"One, two, three, jump," said Nero.

"But is it all right? Are we allowed?" Rosa asked.

He was already up there, looking down with scorn. "*Allowed*? Stop asking foolish questions, Rosa. Just look at these people, they're thrilled with us. That can be very useful. By the way, their names are Robert and Isolde."

"Robert, Isolde," Rosa repeated anxiously.

And Isolde came over, took Rosa on her arm, stroked her, and put her on a pillow next to Nero. "There. Lie next to your little friend."

"You see?" said Nero. "This is how it is. They appreciate us. We'll get everything we could want here, if you just don't act too stupid."

Yes, there they lay, warm and snuggly, purring loudly. Isolde cleared the breakfast table quietly, so as not to disturb them. Robert sat down in a chair opposite his new house companions. He pretended to be paying total attention to the newspaper—but he couldn't fool Don Nero Corleone.

"Yes, well, just look over this way," Nero thought sleepily. "I know what you're thinking. You're thinking, 'Those two are really cute. Are we going to keep them?'" And he said to his dear Rosa, "Looks to me like we have a new home." Then the two cats, happily entwined, fell fast asleep.

Robert and Isolde stayed in their Italian house for almost three weeks. In all that time Nero and Rosa did not leave their sides. At first they still got put outside in the evening so that they could run back to the farm. They did, and ate what Nero disdainfully called "peasant food" again, and then snuggled up in the hay with the other farm cats. But Nero always made sure that bright and early the next morning, before Robert and Isolde got up, he and Rosa were sitting outside the kitchen door, looking oh-so-lonesome, wretched, hungry, and freezing cold, and they were instantly offered a dish of warm milk.

One evening when it was extra cold and not at all cozy outside, Isolde said, "I haven't got the heart to chase them out! You two can sleep here on this little blanket." And she spread a blue-and-red plaid woollen blanket over the green sofa.

Her favorite words were "dear" and "little." "You dear little fellows," "drink a little sweet milk," "lie down on the dear little cat blanket," "I'll leave the little window a little bit open, then you can get out, in case you need to make a little puddle. . . ."

"Oh, for heavens' sake," Nero thought. "She's a good soul, but not too bright." He almost felt sorry for Robert, and thought, "You and me, we're just alike: two clever, capable men of the world, pulling two simple-minded girls along behind us."

The saucers were always filled with good things: sometimes kidneys with rice, then noodles with chopped meat, or beef hearts, pheasant breast, or chicken legs. Nero grew into a splendid tomcat with firm muscles and gleaming fur. Rosa got rounder and rounder, but it became her. She looked a little like a porcelain figurine—white, pink, and light gray, delicate, soft, and, oh my, those squinting sky-blue eyes!

"Look at me straight, my little angel," cried Isolde, laughing. And Rosa would try, but it always seemed more like she was counting the flies on the ceiling.

Back on the farm, Nero liked to tell about the good life over at the vacation house, and just how firmly he had those Germans in his grasp. The animals listened with astonishment, envy, and respect. Sometimes, very politely, they asked his advice.

"Oh my, a boiled egg," sighed Camilla, the fat hen. "I'd so much like to know how that might taste. Don Corleone, do you suppose you could . . . ?"

He could. He brought Camilla a soft-boiled egg, in one piece, exactly as he'd swiped it out of Isolde's eggcup. ("Will you look at the dear little robber, stealing my whole little egg!" Isolde, amused and delighted, had exclaimed.) "There," said Nero. Camilla picked at it, awed and astounded by what had become of this object that she, or a hen just like her, had produced. Meanwhile Nero described to her in detail what boiled chicken legs tasted like.

As the day of Robert and Isolde's departure drew near, Isolde grew quiet and sad, and her eyes were red from crying.

"Can you imagine?" asked Robert. "Ten hours of riding in a car with two cats? And how will it be when we get home?"

Isolde sniffled and blew her nose, and secretly bought a little braided wicker cat-carrier in a housewares store.

Nero suspected that something was about to happen, and he acted exceptionally tender, loving, and affectionate—just to be on the safe side. Isolde had scarcely sat down in the chair for more than a moment when he rolled himself into a ball on her lap and looked up at her soulfully. But he also knew that the most important thing was to convince Robert that life would be empty and meaningless without Rosa and Nero. Tail raised steep and high, he sidled in and out between Robert's legs, peeked coyly out from under the newspaper pages when Robert wanted to read, and showed him his soft, furry belly—meow!

"I see right through you," said Robert, and Nero thought, "Great, then where's the problem?"

He had resolved that, no matter how far they would have to travel, his and Rosa's place was with Robert and Isolde. Room and board would be good, there'd be plenty of affection, and maybe there'd even be hay to sleep in. In any case, they would never again have to fight for every bite of food the way they had to over on the farm. And who knew, maybe there'd be a couch just as butter soft as the one in the vacation house.

One day Robert and Isolde went over to see the farmer. At first they chatted about the weather and politics, about Lothar Matthäus, the famous soccer player, and about how there was nothing worth seeing on TV. And then Isolde came out with it: These two utterly adorable little cats who in recent weeks had come visiting so often, might they, could they perhaps, oh please, take them along? They would most assuredly take good care of them, they had a garden back home and could, as proof, bring photos next time and . . .

"*Due gatti*," asked the farmer, "two cats? Maybe the red one and the black one, *la rosa e il nero?*"

"Yes, yes, that's it," exclaimed Isolde. "Rosa and Nero, that's what we'll call them!"

"*Troppi gatti*, too many cats!" said the farmer, waving them away with his hands. "Many too many cats on this farm. Fine with me, *prendi, prendi*, take them along!"

Isolde wept and threw her arms around Robert's neck, and they all drank a glass of *Riserva del Nonno*, Grandpa's Special Reserve brandy. The farmer's wife tried to get them to take Handsome Felix, too, or how about Biff and Baff? But Robert and Isolde had their hearts set: Rosa and Nero, no others.

Naturally, all this time, Nero had been listening and watching. Now he was strutting around, proclaiming, "Guess what, you hens and cats and dog, I'm going to Germany, the land of Lothar

bridges high as heaven, and through valleys; and Nero and Rosa sat in their carrier, bewildered by the bouncing motion and rushing noises, bitterly

regretting that they'd ever gotten in, and feeling miserable and lost. Rosa whimpered softly and mournfully to herself. Nero screamed as though he were being roasted alive. He started screaming as soon as the car door snapped shut, and didn't stop till the car at long last came to a stop in Cologne on the Rhine, and Isolde and Robert were close to having a nervous breakdown. He screamed piercingly, wickedly, imperiously; he screeched and yowled that he would not stand for being treated thus, that he wanted out where he could poop, which he needed to do, and which he finally did in the cat carrier.

"It stinks," said Robert.

Isolde nearly wept. "They're frightened. Oh my dear little bunnies, just be brave, everything will be all right, my little mice, my sweet little Rosie, my Nero prince."

"Never mind 'Nero prince'!" screamed Nero. "That's stupid stuff, nothing but words. I want out! I can't stand this anymore, I demand better treatment this instant, or the consequences will be dreadful." And he commanded Rosa, "Stop making those pathetic noises: speak up; go ahead, complain, if you don't like it. They shouldn't think they can do as they please with us."

And Rosa sighed, "I feel so bad!"

Every once in a while Robert turned on the stereo to drown out the cats' yowling in the back. And now and then Isolde reached her soft, cool hand inside the carrier to stroke their little heads and give comfort. She fished out Nero's poop with a tissue and threw it out the window. Nero, of course, pretended it was Rosa's poop. But Rosa only let a pitiful little stream of pee seep into the cat blanket on that whole long trip. It was and remained horrendous. And when they arrived in Cologne, they were all at the end of their strength.

But not for long.

While Robert dragged the luggage and boxes of books from the car to the house, Isolde brought the cat carrier into the kitchen, closed all the doors, and set the prisoners free.

"You're home, my little angels," she said. Carefully, Nero and Rosa crept out, and right away a saucer appeared from above with sweet condensed milk in it. Soon they were shown a box lined with crumpled-up paper for peeing in—"Robert, go get some kitty litter, so the little ones can do their business." Clearly a cat could live quite well here.

Nero and Rosa inspected the house. There was a downstairs and an upstairs, nice soft carpets lay on the stairs and in the rooms, and there were many mysterious corners to slip into. Together they crept into the farthest corner underneath the big bed, and began enjoying it very much when Isolde ran all through the house looking for them, loudly crying, "Where can my little treasures be?"

The little treasures thought about their new

life, recovered from the terrors of the journey, and, nestling against each other, sank into a soothing, rejuvenating sleep from which they didn't awake until an indescribably wonderful smell came wafting to their noses. Isolde lay on her stomach and pushed a plate of chopped meat and oatmeal under the bed toward them. "Come, my little rabbits, have something to eat," she coaxed, and the rabbits condescended to dip their bright little tongues into the plate and eat everything up, lickety split.

"They're eating!" Isolde shouted happily, and Robert grumbled, "Naturally, they're gorging themselves. Or did you think they'd go on a hunger strike on account of being homesick for Italy?"

"Sensible fellow," thought Nero again with appreciation. Cleaning his fur, he then emerged dignified from under the bed, ready to explore the rest of his surroundings.

What a disappointment!

One could see out through large windows into a garden with trees, meadows and bushes, birds flying and mice scooting around. But the windows and doors were tightly shut and remained that way.

"No," said Isolde, "my little sweetie-pie has to

stay inside for a good little while, so he won't run off and lose his way. Later, you'll be allowed out."

"'Little sweetie-pie'?" thought Nero angrily. "'Lose my way'? What kind of fur-raising nonsense is that? Why can't I go out into that garden right now? I'm no dummy; why wouldn't I find my way back in?" And he scratched at the terrace door, he insisted and screamed, but for once Isolde did not relent.

"No," she said. "Impossible. First you have to get used to things here, my little rabbit, then you'll be allowed to go outside."

"Little rabbit, little sweetie, little angel, little treasure—" Nero looked disdainfully at Isolde and cursed his decision to go anywhere with these crazy people, to this stupid Germany where gardens lay locked away behind glass panes. What impertinence, what humiliation to be locked in like this! Who did she think he was? By thunder, he was Nero Corleone, the lionheart from Carlazzo, feared by all, and no one could stop him from getting out into his new domain and establishing order!

Nothing doing.

Windows and doors stayed shut, and Nero fell

into sullen brooding. Rosa, after the good meal, had left a big pile of poop in the kitty litter and then climbed into the snow-white featherbed, rolled herself into a ball, and, purring loudly, gone to sleep. Isolde stood before her and pondered whether Rosa squinted even while her eyes were shut. She stroked the little red and white head and whispered, "Sleep well, little Rosa, we love you very much!"

And Nero? Nero trotted through the house, up and down, restless, as furious as Genghis Khan looking for his wild hordes, as Attila, king of the Huns, trying to conquer the world, as . . . well, as a black tomcat eager to announce to his new world out there: *Attention everyone! I am here now! And I am not to be trifled with!*

His hour came the very first night. When Isolde and Robert had finally gone to bed and curved themselves crookedly, uncomfortably around Rosa, Nero noticed that a window in the bedroom was open. Just a narrow slit, but, "You wait," he thought. "I'm about to show you what a rogue your little sweetie-pie really is. Just you go to sleep." And when Robert started snoring, and Isolde sighed and started dreaming of a hundred thousand little cats

for whom she was supposed to cook sweet farina pudding, Nero jumped up on the windowsill, squeezed himself through the narrow slit, and sat outside on the upstairs window ledge.

Aaaaaaah!

Fresh air, night air, with all the sounds and smells a tomcat needs, loves, and wants to know all about. In Italy he knew the sounds of hens scratching—the soft clucking they made in their sleep. He could smell wood fires in farmhouse chimneys, hear moles' high-pitched squeaks and other cats slinking around and even—or so he had imagined—the labored thoughts grinding around in the donkey's head as he tried to solve the world's problems by sheer reflection.

Here, Nero knew nothing—yet. He sat perfectly still, his great green eyes as round as marbles, his tail arranged around his forepaws, his whisker hairs trembling, and his heart beating hard. He did not stir. He listened. He sniffed. He concentrated with all his senses and absorbed his new surroundings.

There had to be a street nearby, for he could hear cars. Lights flitted through the bushes. There must be a hedgehog somewhere, for he heard a low snoring that reminded him of a hedgehog that had hibernated in the farmer's woodpile one winter. And mice were making tiny peep-peep sounds; they were probably smaller mice than the ones back on the farm.

An exquisite odor of ham, meat, and sausage lay in the air, and he could hear a few soft notes from a piano playing somewhere in the distance. The odor was from Bollmann's Delicacies; the notes were the sounds of the composer Kagel, with whose tomcat Nero would later become good friends; but all this he did not yet know. He took in sounds and smells and estimated the height and climbability of the surrounding trees. Could he reach the ground in one leap? Or was it too far? Should he look for someplace in between to jump to?

All this would need thinking about, but he had time. The night was still young, a friendly half moon shone down, and somewhere a clock struck twelve-thirty. You might have thought he was a statue, lifeless, motionless, made of stone, but we know him, don't we? We know that he is warm and soft, and that he's really just gathering strength and courage for his latest great adventure in these strange parts.

Now.

At two o'clock on the dot, he took one giant but precisely calculated leap from the window ledge across into a nearby plum tree. After this first, fabulous feat, he stayed perfectly still again, heart beating hard, for exactly three and a half minutes. Then he climbed down so fast it looked as though a shadow was flitting over the tree, whoosh, right, left, deft, quick, his paws making not a sound—and before you knew it he was down on the cold, stubbly winter lawn and running in great bounds to hide under a hedge. Heart beating. Pride. Excitement. Joy! Grass beneath his paws!

"Hey, Isolde!" he silently shouted up to the high window. "Look, your little rabbit is making a little stream!" And he let the giant lake of pee that he'd been holding in flow under the hedge. When he was finished, and had carefully scrabbled dirt over his work, he took a deep breath and looked around. It was so dark and so quiet that you and I would have seen nothing and heard nothing except for the distant sound of cars. But a tomcat like Nero Corleone could see clearly in that darkness and hear sharply in that silence. He saw earthworms and beetles, he saw birds sleeping on branches, and he heard a thousand kinds of interesting rustlings and stirrings. He was happy. Ah, he had arrived. There'd be plates heaped high with food, and no more worries from here on. As for these new surroundings, he could handle them.

Step by step, over steep and flat, soft and observing, Nero went creeping through his garden and looked at everything very carefully. He caught himself an uninteresting little mouse and ate it up, all except for the paws and the gall bladder. Those he spat out. He licked a little yolk from the eggshells on the neighbor's compost heap. Still not done, he explored the neighbor's garden and the

next one, too. He sat for a while under the Kagels' window, and, in the middle of the night, listened to the soft, strange piano tones.

In the distance he caught sight of a fat tiger tomcat, but he did not feel like getting to know him—not yet, not on his first night. And around seven o'clock in the morning he rolled himself up into a ball on the doormat in front of Robert and Isolde's terrace door and fell asleep, just as the birds in the dark winter sky began to call and flutter.

When Isolde and Robert awoke, there lay Rosa still fast asleep—no longer curled up but stretched out with her forepaws bent and the tip of her little pink tongue sticking out between her teeth. And she snored, very, very softly.

"Oh, how sweet," whispered Isolde, "she's snoring!"

"How come you find it sweet when *she* snores, and if *I* do it you get upset?" asked Robert, stretching his legs because they had gone numb from the cramped position he'd been forced to sleep in thanks to Rosa.

Now Rosa woke, too, gave a big yawn, and sat

up. She wondered where she was.

"Good morning, my precious little snail," said Isolde and stroked her. "That was your first night in Germany!" And Rosa purred and wondered, "Where is Nero?"

Isolde wondered, too. "Where is Nero?" she called, jumping out of bed.

"Nero!" She made clucking, coaxing sounds and ran through the whole house. "Now where can my little mouse be? Make a noise, little prince, come on, say something!"

Her voice got higher and higher and more and more excited. "My little rabbit, where have you hidden yourself?" At that, Robert pulled up the covers and said, "Rosa, what do you say we both catch a few more winks?"

But Rosa was restless. Where was Nero? On soft paws she ran down the stairs, and of course saw him at once: rolled up like a hedgehog, lying on the mat in front of the terrace door with the sun shining on his black fur. Rosa sat by the door and mewed.

"No, my little rabbit heart." Isolde, in her bathrobe, came nearer. "You're not allowed outside.

Look, here's your nice little crate to make pee-pee in, and—oh my goodness!"

She saw Nero and was stunned. "How did you get out into the garden?" she exclaimed, opening the terrace door. Naturally Nero woke up at once, arched his back, yawned, rubbed against Isolde's bare leg, and came strutting, tail held high, into the living room.

"Where's my breakfast?" he demanded, and Isolde knelt on the floor, squeezed him, petted him, and could not understand it. "My little monkey all alone out there in the cold! You need warm milk right away!" She ran into the kitchen, all upset.

"Merciful heaven, the things you get upset about!" thought Nero. "Just kindly warm up the milk and be quick about it."

And that is what Isolde did. She fixed a delicious dish of chopped meat, white bread, and warm milk, and watched them sitting together again, the black tom and his chubby girlfriend who took such joy in eating. Isolde was greatly touched and sighed, "Oh, you good little angels!"

• • •

Little angels? Hardly. Not even Rosa. True, she wasn't very bright, which makes it easier to be good, because you don't think up all kinds of naughty things to do, and, besides, your two favorite activities are eating and sleeping.

But in the next months Rosa turned into a much-feared hunter. She could lie on the lookout for hours, appearing to be asleep, blinking just a bit, with only her ears quivering a little, and then— *zack*! In one leap, with one blow, she'd catch the mouse she'd been watching. And sometimes, unfortunately, she'd catch a little bird not clever or quick enough to escape, and whatever she caught she ate up, hide and hair.

And Nero, having won access to the outside world on his very first night, came and went as he pleased, and it wasn't long before he was boss of the whole neighborhood.

How did he do it? He knew how to win respect: knew when it was better to murmur softly, and when a sharply aimed slap would do the job. And he had such an air about him that no one within the boundaries of his domain argued or resisted.

Old black-and-white spotted Klara, who belonged to Grandma Riegert, had never seen such an elegant tom, and oh how she wished that she were a little bit younger.

Frau Brettschneider's snow-white tom, Timmi, ran away the moment he saw Nero.

The Hahns' little Amadeus always left a few pieces of food on his plate for Nero, just to stay on his good side.

Fräulein von Kleist's silver-gray Carthusian, who'd won prizes in nearly every cat show, and who was never allowed outside, sat gazing out the window at Nero, longing for him with all her heart and soul.

And with the Kagels' tomcat, Karl, Nero soon

forged a firm friendship: together they strolled through the garden or over the rooftops and discussed matters of importance. When the Kagels went traveling—which was often—Karl and Nero sat whole nights long in their deep leather armchairs, like two old men smoking cigars. Or else they ran together over the piano keys and made splendid modern music.

Diagonally across from Nero's domain lived Tiger, a rather strong tomcat who belonged to a school teacher. It was with Tiger that Nero had trouble.

On their first encounter, Tiger laid back his ears. His fur stood on end, and he hissed, "Get lost!"

Nero just looked at him and said, "Tiger, you've got gumption, I can see that. You're not made of Jell-O, and you aren't spoiled like the other pussycats running around here. You and I could beat each other bloody, but that wouldn't end well for you. So, let's agree that you don't enter my domain, and I don't enter yours, okay, Stripes?"

"Are you for real?" Tiger hissed again. "You have some nerve. You've only just got here, and you already think you have a domain?" Evil-tempered, itching to give this Italian tough guy a couple of smacks in the face, Tiger came stealthily nearer.

"Tiger, Tiger, you're being presumptuous," said Nero very quietly, as if nothing was wrong, and he polished his black fur with his white paw.

"Didn't you hear what I said before?" snarled Tiger. "Get lost. Beat it, go on."

"Pussycat, please change your tone of voice. I warn you: In Italy they called me Corleone, which means Lionheart. There I was—well, shall we say, important, famous—"

"And if you were the emperor of China"—Tiger had picked up an education of sorts, living with a school teacher; he knew about emperors, China, and all sorts of things—"you still wouldn't impress me, you with your black monkey fur."

Nero laid himself down on the ground, quite flat, and did not move. Only his tail jerked this way and that. "Monkey fur?" he asked in a mild tone. "Did you say 'monkey fur,' you strangely striped sausage?" Then he sprang, quick as a thought, at Tiger's neck and gave him a good, sharp bite.

Tiger cried out. Nero loosened his toothhold a

little and growled, "Did you really say 'monkey fur' just now, or could I have misheard?"

"You misheard!" screeched Tiger, and the teacher appeared on the balcony and called, "Tiger? Is anything wrong?"

"Your little mama is calling," Nero said, and let go of Tiger, who rushed off and ran up his ladder to the second floor, where the teacher received him with a frightened, "Oh no, you're bleeding!"

Tiger needed four stitches, and for the next ten days he had to wear a humiliating ruffled kerchief around his neck, which made him a laughingstock throughout the neighborhood. From then on, whenever he saw Nero, he ran quickly to his teacher, and Nero spat disdainfully and grumbled, "Mama's boy."

One mild summer night, Nero succeeded in luring Fräulein von Kleist's beautiful, purebred Carthusian out into the open. "Hello, little Kleistie," he called and called in his sweetest voice. Her heart swelled, then it melted. And not long thereafter, she proudly showed five newborn kittens to her owner: three black ones, and two

gray ones. Fräulein von Kleist was flabbergasted, outraged. For the Carthusian's family tree went back to the twelfth century, and something like this was simply not allowed!

No, not allowed, but it happened all the same, because no one can get in the way of true love. Little Kleistie pleased Nero very much, and vice versa. These five children of theirs were merely the beginning.

Soon there were others, including pure snow-white ones and quite a few jet-black ones whose boldness did honor to their father. They all found homes with more or less good families all over Marienburg, Bayenthal, Zollstock, all the way up toward Klettenberg.

Sometimes when the moon shone, Nero lured his little Kleistie out of her house and climbed up on the roofs with her. Then they gazed at the moon, sang a little, and he cooed, "Little Kleistie, I tell you, life is beautiful!"

And she answered, "Yes, yes, and next week you'll have someone new."

Nero looked at her reproachfully, showed her both his forepaws—the white one and the black one—and said in a honey-sweet voice, "I beg you, little Kleistie, look. Can these paws stray?" And then she had to laugh, and they sang on for another little while.

Now and then the other cats brought Nero a little mouse (or at least the tastier half of one), or saved him a few cat biscuits. Karlheinz even asked him for protection.

Karlheinz was a scruffy old tom with a cough and only one eye. He lived outdoors on his own, strolled through gardens, rifled through garbage cans, found things to eat here and there, and knew two or three addresses where, at one time or another, he'd received a plate of food and been allowed to sleep down in the cellar.

"Listen," Karlheinz said to Nero. "If you were to keep that disreputable Tiger away from me, and also General Grabowski's wife's idiotic dog, I could, now and then, tell you where a bowl of soup has been set out to cool, or something."

The arrangement worked well. Nero took care of General Grabowski's wife's dog, and a few days later, in exchange, Karlheinz came sidling over to Nero, and revealed: "At Number 20, directly in front of the dentist's lovely wife's kitchen door, there's a boiled chicken cooling off for chicken salad."

"Thanks, my friend," said Nero, already on his way. And he left some of the chicken over for Karlheinz, too! And he never failed to bring a tasty morsel home to his Rosa, especially when he returned from Bollmann's Delicacies.

Only rich people shopped at Bollmann's: women in fur coats, dressed to kill. Fur coats—Nero loathed and detested them. He took deep, personal offense at the sight of so much dead animal hair. And then there were the gentlemen who came to buy lobster and champagne—perfumed dandies in double-breasted jackets. Double-breasted! Nero couldn't stand those.

Ah, but in the store were scrumptious patés, delicate smoked salmon, truffled sausages, and the finest fish filets. To reach them, you only had to get inside the cooling room. And that required getting past a dog. But that dog, thanks to a lifelong diet of the store's finest delicacies, was sluggish, slow, and dopey.

Nero had introduced the dog to his white paw, explaining very clearly what the paw could do to a dog's eyesight, then earnestly requested that the

hens. He heard the silvery leaves of the olive trees rustling, and he remembered the bed where the farmer had planted catnip.

Home! When all was said and done, *tutti santi in colonna*, by all the saints on all the columns, he was Italian, he was old, he was tired, and all he wanted was to go home.

He knew that now he'd have to pussyfoot around Isolde, purr his hardest, make her happy in every way, so she'd let him come along. For he'd learned this much in all these years: in such matters, Robert had absolutely no say. Sure, he had opinons on weighty matters: things like whether the Americans were right or wrong to get mixed up in Haiti, whether or not to vote for the Green party, whether the American dollar was rising or falling, and whether the Austrian writer Peter Handke was truly great or not. But it was up to Isolde to decide what to cook for dinner, whether to have a Christmas tree, when and where to travel, and whether cats should sleep in beds or not. (They should.)

Isolde decided that Nero would come along to Italy. No need to hire Frau Wiegand this time. They locked up the house. And Nero resigned himself to his fate: ten hours in the little carrier.

He gave a deep sigh, rolled himself tightly into a ball, and fell asleep without a single complaint. He dreamed about the first trip, so long ago, with his little Rosa. He dreamed of Italian nights with the sky much bluer and the stars much nearer than in Germany. He dreamed of fragrant woodsmoke rising from the chimneys, and of his mother, Madonnina, whom he hadn't thought about for fifteen years.

"Mamma," he thought, "Mamma, your little son is coming home."

But Madonnina, of course, was no longer alive. After they arrived, and after a bowl of good, nourishing meat, Nero made his way carefully down the hill and through the meadow. The clock on the church steeple of Carlazzo chimed one of its off-key melodies, and Nero ducked behind the hazelnut hedge and gazed over at the farm.

The farmer, grown old and bent, was just scattering corn for the hens, among whom a big, multi-colored rooster now strutted. Nero kept his eyes peeled for somebody familiar, but the stupid hens all looked alike to him. Even back when he'd lived here he hadn't been able to tell them apart. He heard no barking—clearly, no more dog. He saw various cats flitting around or lying lazily on the roofs of sheds and on the chicken coop. He didn't know them, yet they seemed familiar—gray ones, black and white ones, red and white ones, clearly children or grandchildren of Madonnina. Madonnina, though, he did not see.

At dusk, he nodded off in the grass midway between the two houses: the farmhouse where he had been born and the house on the hill that belonged to the people with whom he'd lived a good, long, tomcat life.

Isolde had opened the windows wide and was busy unpacking while listening to loud music by Rossini.

"*The Tomcat*, by Rossini," Nero thought sleepily. "He should have composed an opera about someone like me. That would have been something." Because of course Rossini was not only a wonderful Italian composer but also a magnificent chef. *Tournedos à la Rossini* still bear his name to this day. The combination of great music and great food was something that Nero Corleone found irresistible. Isolde cooked well enough and generously, but without refinement. Ah well, what with

Bollmann's Delicacies, he'd always managed to provide himself with everything necessary for luxurious living.

All of that he thought about, there behind the hazelnut hedge, gazing at his old farm home that seemed to him smaller than back then, and yet so familiar.

Suddenly somebody nudged him. It gave him a terrible scare, for never before had anyone sneaked up unnoticed on the great, ever-watchful Corleone. Fur bristling, he jumped up, whipped out his claws, and looked into the loveliest, roundest, amber-colored eyes he'd ever seen; into the small, gray, darling face of an enchanting little wonderfully beautiful young cat. There she sat, right before him, well behaved and friendly, and purred in a sweet, soft voice, "Well, who might you be?"

Oh, it was love at first sight! A pitiful wretch is he who has never felt it. It's like . . . yes, like what? Like a lightning bolt, a burst of thunder; the heart trembles, the paws grow cold and the feet do, too, because all the blood flows into the heart. It makes a stupid thud-thud-thudding inside the head, and there is not a thing that can be done about it; a sim-

pering smile just spreads over the face. That is what
happened to our Nero Corleone at the sight of this
little gray cat with the gentle, starlike eyes. Ice-
cold paws, glowing heart, a choking sensation. "I
am . . ." he wanted to say, but it sounded like raw
coughing, and so he pretended he had to clear his
throat and lay back down. "I am I," he said haugh-
tily, but his voice trembled. "And who are you?"

"I am Grigiolina [gree-jo-leen-a]; it's what they
call me over there—it means 'the little gray one.'"

"You're from over there?" he asked, his white paw pointing to the farm.

Grigiolina nodded. "Yes. And do you know something? They're always talking about someone from long ago who was all black except for one white paw, who got involved in all kinds of dark doings—" She burst into merry laughter. "He must have looked a lot like you, but he moved away to Germany many years ago."

Nero looked attentively at Grigiolina. She had Madonnina's eyes, she had Rosa's dear face, and her beautiful fur was a lot like little Kleistie's—oh how much in love he was! What should he answer her? Always so quick-witted, never at a loss before, why couldn't he think of a single thing to say?

"Go on, tell me more," he begged.

"Oh," she mewed and flicked her little rough tongue gently over Nero's head, which made him shudder, "there's not much to tell. It's just that they all talk about him. I heard about him from my mamma, she heard about him from her mamma, the donkey knew him, and there's a very old hen, Camilla, who remembers him well. They called him Don Nero Corleone."

She polished her fur and his, too. She purred

and looked at him sweetly. "And you," she asked, "what is your name?"

Nero sighed deeply and closed his eyes. His heart beat so loud it seemed it would burst. His whole life appeared before him, the past as well as the future: his youth on the farm, the years in Germany where he had found friends, and the notion of growing old back here by the side of this enchanting little cat.

"Grigiolina," he said earnestly, purring his deepest, far down in his throat, and laying his white paw firmly on the gray cat's little head, "run over there, quick, and tell everybody: Don Nero Corleone has returned."

For the next several days Nero scarcely left the house on the hill. He couldn't yet. He wasn't ready. He was afraid. Of what? Well, if he only knew exactly . . . Afraid of what sort of reception they'd give him over there; of seeing Grigiolina again; of having to start his life all over again; of giving up everything he had become used to—the rugs, the soft couches, warm beds, and well-filled saucers. And Isolde's lap. Isolde!

"He's never acted so clingy before," said

Isolde, touched, while Robert, reading an exceptionally thick new novel, pondered once again whether its author, Peter Handke, was truly a great writer or not.

"What did you say?" he asked.

"He's so clingy," said Isolde. "Ever since Rosa died, he hasn't budged from my side, have you, Nero, my little prince?" She stroked his black head and buried her nose between his ears. "You and I," she said softly, "we'll always stay together."

Nero's heart shuddered with love and grief. He heaved a deep sigh. "No, dearest," he thought, "we won't."

Then he sprang off her lap and went outside. He ran over to the farm right away. He slipped under the fence and stood there, right near the herb bed where the catnip once grew. He recognized everything—the haystacks, the grapevines, and the olive trees. The doghouse still stood there, with the chain still there, but it was empty. Nero hadn't liked the dog, but—it was strange—now he almost missed him. "Old boy," he thought, "you're probably in dog heaven, annoying everybody with your barking."

A gray-and-white striped tom came menacingly toward him, ears laid back, tail bristling, ready for a fight. He gave a low, ominous growl. Nero made the striped tom nervous by just standing quietly and letting him approach.

"Hey you, beat it," snarled the tom, but came no closer.

"No," said Nero in an amicable but determined tone, "on the contrary, I'm just arriving. You'd do better not to act like a big shot with me, considering you don't know who I am, *d'accordo*, do you understand?" And, head raised high, he simply strode past the young, strong tom and continued on, not looking back.

Now I'll tell this just to *you*, but let it go no further: Nero was a little bit scared. He didn't feel quite as big on the inside as he pretended to be on the outside, if you know what I mean. He wasn't sure what he would have done if that striped tom had gotten angry and jumped on his back.

But nothing like that happened. The tom just sat there dumbfounded, and Nero made his entrance into his farm. The hens looked up from their pecking, and an age-old, rumpled, withered one came limping toward him and looked at him with one eye for a long while—the other eye was blind.

"Corleone," she squawked, "have you come home? I knew you'd be back. I have never forgotten that you once brought me a soft-boiled egg."

"Camilla," said Nero, greatly moved, "and you didn't land in the soup?"

"As you see," Camilla giggled, "too tough, too tough."

Suddenly Grigiolina came leaping along.

"Here you are!" she cried, excited. "I told everybody about you. Welcome home!" And she licked him all over his face. The other cats came nearer, carefully, but not looking unfriendly.

"I knew your mother," said a black and white one. "She was very proud of you and often spoke of you. What did you do in Germany?"

"This and that," said Nero, "business and so on. Now I'm tired and want to have my rest."

"Just don't act like a big shot," muttered the gray-and-white striped tom, displeased. "You're not the king around here."

Nero turned his head at an angle and stared at him for so long that the gray-and-white striped tom started feeling less sure of himself.

"What's your name?" asked Nero.

"The farmer calls me Mascalzone." That means scoundrel.

"Good name." Nero nodded, approving. "When I was your age, I acted just like you. But don't forget who you're dealing with. Just make sure you never get to feel this white paw of mine," he warned, showing it to Mascalzone. "*Va bene*, understood?"

Mascalzone stuck his tail between his legs and slunk away. "You're just the same as always," cackled the half-blind hen Camilla, and was delighted.

"Come," said Grigiolina, "I'll show you a fine place in the hay where you can sleep."

And she went with him and sat down beside him in the hayloft, near a gap in the wall which afforded a good view of the village of Carlazzo and of the whole farm.

Toward evening the farmer came with a big metal plate of food for the cats. Nero didn't go down. "Bring me something," he said to Grigiolina, and she sprang away and came back with a beautiful hunk of meat.

"The farmer is friendly," she said. "He won't chase you away. It's all right to go down."

"Not yet," said Nero. "I have my reasons." And he gazed into her gentle eyes. "You look like someone I used to love very much," he said, and Grigiolina purred happily.

That night, Nero returned one more time to the house on the hill. He stole into Isolde's bed, and she said sleepily, "So here you are, my little monkey. I've been looking for you. Where were you?"

Nero squeezed himself tight against Isolde's leg and purred. She went back to sleep, but not he. He lay awake till morning and thought of all the saucers she had filled with food for him. He thought of her hand that had stroked him a thousand times, of the stupid names she'd given him—

for love. For love. He thought of the visits to the veterinarian when he was sick, of the ointment she'd made for his paw when a bee had stung him, and of all the little paper balls that she had rolled across the floor to him on boring, rainy days. He thought of how she'd always called to him, first thing, when she came home. And he listened to Robert softly snoring and thought of all the times Robert had pinched him playfully and said, "Hey there, old boy" to him.

"Farewell," he thought.

It grew light in the room. Isolde's hand hung down over the edge of the bed. Nero licked it with his rough tongue, but ever so gently. He stuck his nose deep into her blue velvet slipper one last time. Then he climbed out through the open window and ran over to the farm, just as the cock began to crow.

Four days and four nights he lay hidden in the hay, ate nothing, said nothing, didn't want to see anybody except Grigiolina, who worried about him. Four days and four nights he heard Isolde calling him—sometimes near, sometimes far, sometimes down in the valley, sometimes up on the mountain. And she called him by all the stupid names—"My little prince, my little angel, my little bunny. Oh my Nero, where are you?"

He didn't budge. And he didn't stir when she came to the farm and asked the farmer about him.

No, said the farmer, he had not seen Nero, whom he'd surely recognize at once. Yes, of course he would let her know if Nero turned up. Isolde cried and left.

Nero stuck his head still deeper into the hay.

Then the shutters were closed over there, and boxes and suitcases were packed into the car. One last time Nero heard Isolde tearfully calling his name.

When the car drove off, he crept out of the hay, climbed up onto the roof, and followed it with milky eyes till it vanished in the curve behind the church.

"*Arrivederci,*" he murmured, "Isolde, farewell, *ciao. Roberto, ragazzo mio,* old boy, take good care of our girl. You know how helpless she is without us."

And then he went down to the farm.

The farmer was digging in his garden beds. His eyes grew round when he saw Nero.

"You Satan," he said. Only that. They looked